rabbit ears

First published in the United States of America in March 2006
by Bloomsbury Books for Young Readers
Paperback edition published in February 2012
www.bloomsburykids.com

For information about permission to reproduce selections from this book, write to
Permissions, Bloomsbury BFYR, 175 Fifth Avenue, New York, New York 10010

The Library of Congress has cataloged the hardcover edition as follows:
Stewart, Amber.
Rabbit ears / Amber Stewart ; illustrated by Laura Rankin.
p.   cm.
Summary: Hopscotch the rabbit refuses to wash his ears until his
older cousin comes to visit and he learns something about being grown up.
ISBN-10: 1-58234-959-2 · ISBN-13: 978-1-58234-959-6 (hardcover)
[1. Baths—Fiction. 2. Ear—Fiction. 3. Cleanliness—Fiction. 4. Rabbits—Fiction.]
I. Rankin, Laura, ill. II. Title.
PZ7.S84868Rab 2006   [E]—dc22   2005054578

ISBN 978-1-59990-740-6 (paperback)

Art created with acrylic inks and paints on Arches watercolor paper
Typeset in Cheltenham Light
Design by Filomena Tuosto

Printed in China by C&C Offset Printing Co., Ltd., Shenzhen, Guangdong
3 5 7 9 10 8 6 4 2

FSC
www.fsc.org
MIX
Paper from
responsible sources
FSC® C008047

rabbit ears

Amber Stewart

illustrated by Laura Rankin

BLOOMSBURY

NEW YORK BERLIN LONDON SYDNEY

To my very lovely Lottie and Josh
I love you—clean ears or not
—A.S.

For Tyler and Ryan
—L.R.

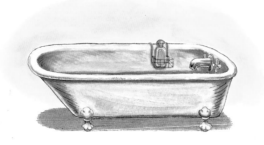

Hopscotch knew what he liked and what he did not like.

He did like Rabbity,

building a tower
twelve blocks high
with no wobbles at all,

and very chocolaty chocolate cake
(with extra icing on the side).

Hopscotch did not like
lumpy pudding,

cold wet paws,

and losing Rabbity just before bedtime, even though Rabbity
was usually found exactly where Hopscotch had left him.

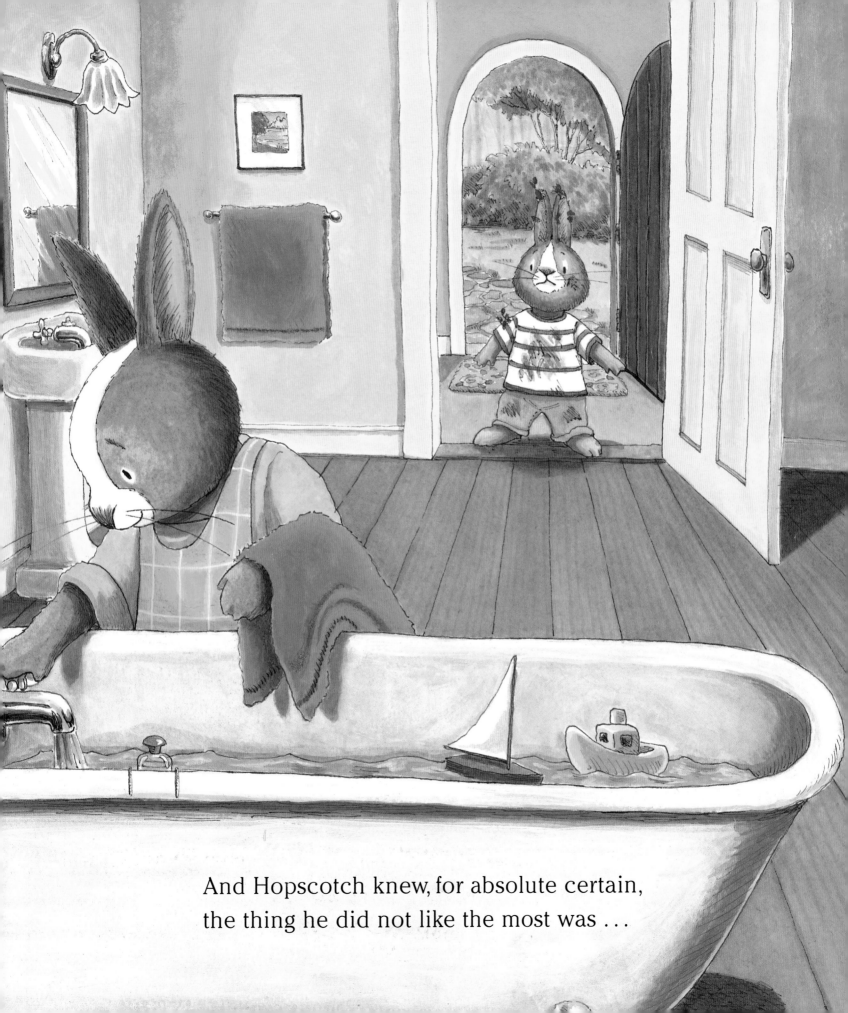

And Hopscotch knew, for absolute certain,
the thing he did not like the most was ...

...having his ears washed!

Hopscotch liked his ears dry.
He did not like them soapy.
The soap always ran away, then ended up
in his nose and made him sneeze.
The sneezes shook him from
his soggy, drippy ears to his toes.
Hopscotch didn't like it one little bit.

Hopscotch would do a lot not to have his ears washed.

With Rabbity's help, he would hide them.

Sometimes he'd pretend that he had suddenly turned into a cat—a cat with very small, clean ears.

Or he would hold on to them very, very tightly.

Hopscotch's mother tried tricking him ...
"Where's the airplane?"

Hopscotch's mother tried begging him ...
"Please, just this once?"

She even tried chocolate cake . . .
"Look, it's your favorite."
But nothing worked.

One day, Hopscotch's big cousin Bobtail
came to stay—just for one day and a night.

Hopscotch and Bobtail played high jump, long jump.

Then they listened for danger as they rescued Rabbity from the lion's den.

They played and played until all too soon it was suppertime.

"When can I go and stay all by myself at Bobtail's?" asked Hopscotch through a mouthful of extra-chocolaty chocolate cake.

"When you are big, little Hopscotch," said Daddy.
"When you are big." After supper, it was time for a bath.

Hopscotch was happily playing submarines
when he noticed something odd . . .

Bobtail was washing his own ears!

He didn't seem to mind the runaway soap.

Not one bit.

And he didn't get the sneezes at all.

Not one sneeze.

"Big rabbits wash their own ears," thought Hopscotch.

Hopscotch felt it might be a good idea
to practice ear-washing on Rabbity first.
Rabbity didn't seem to mind it at all—
in fact, they had fun with all the bubbles.

"What are you up to, Hopscotch?" asked Daddy.

"I'm practicing," said Hopscotch.

"Practicing what?" asked Daddy.

"Practicing washing my ears so I can be big and go
 and stay with Bobtail all by myself," said Hopscotch.

"Well," said Daddy, "that's wonderful!"

Hopscotch knew what he liked and what he *really* liked.
He liked bathtime with Rabbity and clean soapy ears.

He *really* liked singing a song with Mommy
to celebrate his very clean ears.

Soapy, soapy, soapy ears, soapy ears,
soapy ears
Washy, washy, washy ears, washy ears,
washy ears
Fluffy, fluffy, fluffy ears, fluffy ears,
fluffy ears
All day long!

And best of all, he liked
packing his favorite games,

waving good-bye to Mommy and Daddy,

and going to stay with big cousin Bobtail for one
whole day and a night all by himself. Well, almost...

Rabbity came too.